Weekly Reader Children's Book Club Presents

I KNOW A PLACE

KAREN ACKERMAN

Illustrated by

DEBORAH KOGAN RAY

Houghton Mifflin Company

Boston 1992

This book is a presentation of Newfield Publications, Inc.
Newfield Publications offers book clubs for children from
preschool through high school. For further information
write to: **Newfield Publications, Inc.,** 4343 Equity Drive,
Columbus, Ohio 43228.

Published by arrangement with Houghton Mifflin Company.
Newfield Publications is a federally registered trademark of
Newfield Publications, Inc. Weekly Reader is a federally
registered trademark of Weekly Reader Corporation.

Library of Congress Cataloging-in-Publication Data

Ackerman, Karen, 1951-
  I know a place / Karen Ackerman: Illustrated by Deborah Kogan Ray.
        p.   cm.
  Summary: A child describes a place where all the rooms have warmth,
comfort and love, and it turns out to be home.
  ISBN 0-395-53932-3
  [1. Home—Fiction. 2. Dwellings—Fiction.] I. Ray, Deborah Kogan,
1940-   ill. II. Title.
PZ7.A1824Iak   1991   90-46548
[E]—dc20   CIP
                    AC

For Kelly and Cammy,
and in tender memory of
Lisa Steinberg—K.A.

I know a place
where the sound of slippers in the hall
means "Rise and shine, lazybones!"

and ribbons of sun stream through the blinds,
warming the rush from pj's to jeans.

I know a place
where pillows are fluffed, bedcovers smoothed,
and stray clothes picked up from the floor.

Pots and pans clang in the kitchen,
sweet with the smell of toasted muffins.

I know a place
where the school bus honks too early,
and milk spills in a race for the door.

Wet boots go on the back mat at three,
and a gold-starred paper wins a smile.

I know a place
where there's homework to do at the counter,
and the table is set for supper at six.

The dishes might be chipped or cracked,
but there's never been an empty one.

I know a place
where early evening is for being together,
and the fire warms a row of stockinged feet.

A favorite old movie is on TV,
and popcorn on the stove goes *Pop! Ping! Pop!*

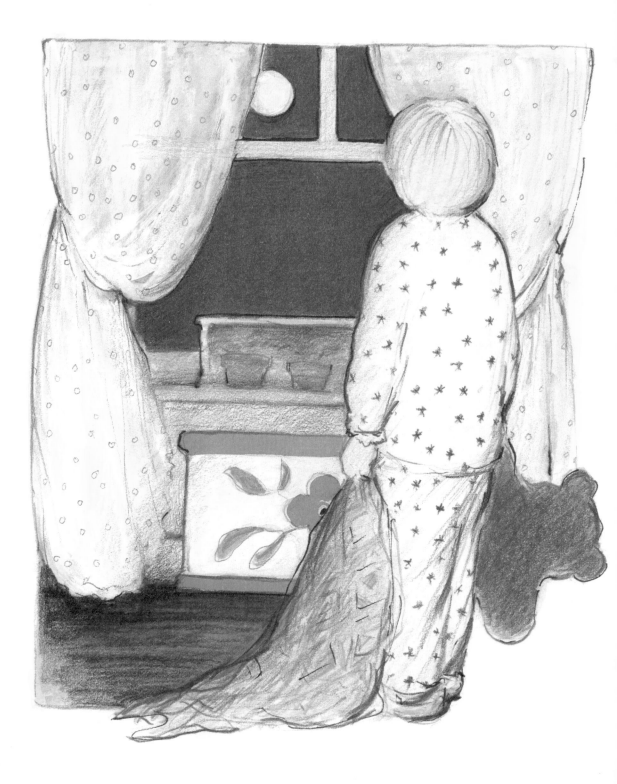

I know a place
where a white winter moon shines outside,
and a hand-me-down quilt is just right inside
for snuggling down to hear a story
that's read softly as a lullaby.

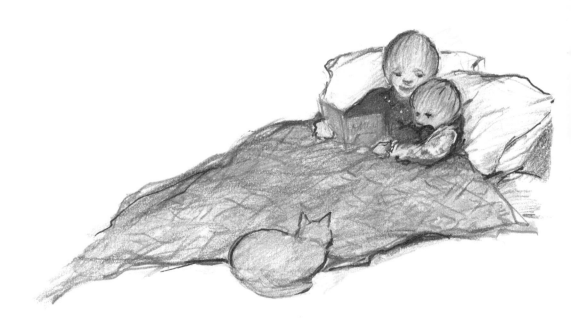

I know a place
where a clock in the hall tick-tocks the hours
like the even breathing of a quiet night,

and Dark means open doors, friendly creakings,
or sharing the covers with a one-eyed bear.

I know a place, and I know it by heart —
by the number and by the street —

Home.